Mixed-up Magic

FAIRY SCHOOL

Mixed-up Magic

by Gail Herman

illustrated by Fran Gianfriddo

A Skylark Book

New York · Toronto · London · Sydney · Auckland

RL: 2.5, AGES 006–009

MIXED-UP MAGIC

A Bantam Skylark Book / January 2000

ISBN: 0-375-80605-9

Visit us on the Web! www.randomhouse.com/kids

Educators and librarians, for a variety of teaching tools, visit us at www.randomhouse.com/teachers

Published simultaneously in the United States and Canada

Bantam Skylark is an imprint of Random House Children's Books, a division of Random House, Inc. SKYLARK BOOKS, BANTAM BOOKS, and the rooster colophon are registered trademarks of Random House, Inc. Bantam Books, 1540 Broadway, New York, New York 10036.

PRINTED IN THE UNITED STATES OF AMERICA

CWO   10 9 8 7 6 5 4 3 2 1

To Jeff, for our many mix-ups!

Chapter 1

"Oh, where is it?" Dorrie said. She pushed her long, unruly curls from her face and looked around her tree-house bedroom.

The little fairy, three inchworms high, sorted through books, feather pens, and odds and ends, making a jumble of all her belongings.

"Dorrie Lucinda Windmist!" she scolded herself. "This is the third time this week you've lost your fairypack. Now you're going to be late again."

Practically every morning, Dorrie met Trina Larkspur, Olivia Skye, and Belinda Dentalette under the weeping willow tree in Fairyland Meadow so that they could fly to Fairy School together. Today they were supposed to get there early. Trina was going to help Dorrie practice for the school talent show. Their class was performing the "Dance of the Sugar Plum Fairy," and Dorrie was worried about making mistakes.

"I am so clumsy," she moaned. "I can't be late. I need all the extra dance practice I can get!"

She remembered rehearsal the day before. She had bumped into other fairies, fallen down, and crashed into a wall of leaves.

And if that wasn't bad enough, the dance was supposed to end with a magical spell in which students waved their wands to make a rainbow. But Dorrie had held her wand upside down, and the whole rainbow had turned a horrid black.

Trina's help was so important!

Just then Dorrie's taller sister, Arianna, flew into the room. She was in the fourth grade. The sisters were as different as sunlight and starlight. Arianna was graceful, just like their parents. She never bumped into things or fell down. Dorrie wished she were more like her.

Dorrie scurried around the room, looking for her fairypack. She tripped over her fairy sneakers and tumbled to the ground right in front of her sister.

"Maybe if you cleaned up your mess, you wouldn't fall so much." Arianna gazed down at Dorrie. "Good fairies never lose their balance."

"I can fall and still be a good fairy," Dorrie told her sister as she scrambled to her feet.

"Name one good fairy who's clumsy," Arianna challenged.

3

Dorrie thought and thought and thought some more. She couldn't think of one clumsy fairy. Tall or little. "Ummm . . ."

"Exactly," said Arianna. "If you want to be a good fairy, you'd better be neat. And try not to fall all the time either."

"Cuckoo!" A cuckoo-clock bird flew past the window.

"Time flies," Arianna warned her little sister. "Better hurry if you want to meet your friends!" And off she flew.

Dorrie jumped. "Where is that fairypack? I can't leave without it—I need my wand for the dance."

Maybe it had rolled into Arianna's closet.

Dorrie didn't want to open the closet. Arianna would be mad if she looked through her stuff. But what choice did Dorrie have? She had looked everywhere else.

Moving oh so carefully, Dorrie opened the

closet. Suddenly handfuls of fairy dust spilled out of a sweater pocket.

"Oh, no!" she cried. "I'm making a mess!"

Immediately she clapped a wing over her mouth. Thoughts guided fairy dust. And now that she had said "mess," who knew what would happen?

Sure enough, the fairy dust swirled around the room. Clothes flew out of the closet, and shoes whirled in figure eights. Books tumbled to the ground. Seashell combs clattered to the floor. Arianna's raindrop ring bounced under the leaf-bed.

Hurriedly Dorrie piled everything back in its place. She scooted under the bed, grabbed the ring, and put it back.

And there, right on top of Arianna's dresser, was Dorrie's fairypack! "How did you get there?" she wondered out loud. Before anything else could happen, she grabbed her bag and rushed to meet her friends.

Chapter 2

A few minutes later, Dorrie flew to the weeping willow tree in Fairyland Meadow.

"Boo-hoo!" cried the tree. "Your friends aren't here yet, and I have a knot in my branches!"

Dorrie must have flown as fast as Belinda, the fastest fairy in the whole first grade, to beat her friends. She grinned. At least she'd done one thing right this morning!

"I'll help you, Mr. Willow," she offered. She gently untangled his drooping branches.

"Thank you." The willow sighed. "That mean Laurel is here, and she didn't lift one wing to help."

"What's Laurel doing here?" Dorrie asked.

"Take a peek," the willow suggested.

Dorrie moved aside a branch, making sure it didn't get tangled again, and spied Laurel under the tree. Laurel dipped into a pretty curtsy, then rose up on her toes, fluttering her wings.

"She's dancing!" Dorrie whispered. Maybe I should go away, she thought, and come back when my friends get here. Laurel was mean and bossy, and Dorrie tried to stay far away from her. But watching her, Dorrie found herself rooted to the spot—just like the weeping willow tree.

Laurel was practicing the "Dance of the Sugar Plum Fairy." She was a beautiful dancer. Maybe I could learn something from her, Dorrie thought. She watched Laurel twirl and spin, then soar into the air, at last drifting down to land gently.

Dorrie rose too, swooping under the branches to copy Laurel's steps. But her wings got caught in the leaves. Suddenly she plunged to the ground, falling in a heap at Laurel's feet.

Laurel jumped in surprise and tripped over a root. She tottered dangerously—right above a sharp rock.

"Oh! Watch out!" Dorrie cried. She rushed to her feet and grabbed Laurel, holding her tight until she got her balance. "You almost fell!" Dorrie said, smiling. "I know what that's like!"

Embarrassed, Laurel turned the color of the reddest sunset. "A lot you know!" she retorted. "I did that on purpose! And how dare you spy on me!"

"I wasn't spying. You looked so pretty, I just wanted to watch."

"Humph!" Laurel turned up her nose at Dorrie. Then she rushed away, just as Trina flew under the weeping willow tree.

"Hi, Dorrie," Trina said in her serious way. "Laurel looked as mean as ever. Are you ready to practice?"

Dorrie didn't answer. She stood still as a statue, thinking about Laurel. She didn't even blink when Belinda and Olivia darted next to her.

"Hello!" Belinda said, knocking lightly on Dorrie's wing. "Anyone home?"

Dorrie laughed, and Olivia grinned. "That's better. For a minute I thought I was home with the twins, playing fairy freeze-tag."

"I was just wondering where Laurel rushed off to," Dorrie explained. She would have liked to watch Laurel dance some more.

"You should be happy she's gone," said Belinda.

Dorrie remembered every rotten thing Laurel had done to her friends. How Laurel had teased Belinda about being a terrible tooth fairy. How she had tried to win the cloud-shaping contest so that Olivia—a very talented artist—wouldn't.

Then Dorrie pictured Laurel's graceful curtsy. Mean or not, Laurel could really dance!

Chapter 3

The four little fairies practiced the "Dance of the Sugar Plum Fairy" under Mr. Willow. Dorrie had a hard time getting it right. She turned left when she should have turned right. She bowed when she should have soared. And she tripped over a rock when she tried to balance on one toe. Still, she had fun with her friends.

Laughing and talking, the fairies flew to

their school-tree. A few minutes later, Ms. Periwinkle led the first-grade students in the Fairy School Pledge. Dorrie stood by her toadstool-desk, singing with the others. She loved the pledge. It made her feel important to sing it every day.

After the pledge, Dorrie took out her tooth fairy textbook, ready for class.

Ms. Periwinkle smiled. "No tooth fairy class this morning. It's such a nice day, I thought we'd have a special wish-granting class in the school meadow. That way, we can work on our wand-waving for the big finish of the Sugar Plum Fairy dance. I think everyone's wand work can be improved."

Laurel wheeled around to glare at Dorrie. "She means you!" she hissed.

Dorrie blushed as a few other students turned to look at her too. She knew she was the one who needed the most practice.

Well, at least I've got my wand, Dorrie

thought. She reached into her fairypack . . . and the wand wasn't there!

"Oh, no," she groaned. "I must have dropped it under Mr. Willow!"

She'd lost something again!

Ms. Periwinkle fluttered closer. "Don't worry, Dorrie. You can borrow this." She handed Dorrie a long, thin wand.

"Thank you," Dorrie said uncertainly. This wand felt a little strange—much lighter than her own.

I hope I can make it work, she thought.

Dorrie flitted outside with her class. She didn't get very far before she tangled her wings in a hanging vine. She tumbled free, then landed on the soft grass with a thud.

"Oops!" She dropped the wand. "No one move!" she called. "I don't want anyone to step on my wand."

She shifted from one foot to the other, looking around. *Crunch!*

Dorrie gasped. She bent close to the ground, and there was the wand—broken in half.

Ms. Periwinkle hovered above her. "That's all right, Dorrie," she said gently. "We'll find you another after I start the rest of the fairies on their spells."

She clapped her wings for everyone's attention. "Now, class, let's start waving those wands. Remember—to grant a wish, you have to think about something someone else wants and wave your wand. Speak your spell out loud and in rhyme. The best wishes are those you want from the bottom of your heart."

"And you know that wishes granted here won't last," Ms. Periwinkle reminded the class. "As soon as class is over, the spells are broken. Olivia, why don't you begin?"

Olivia nodded, then stepped next to Dorrie. *"Dorrie's wand just broke in two. Now come together, good as new."*

A Band-Aid floated down from the sky and wrapped itself around Dorrie's wand. "Well, that's not really good as new!" Olivia exclaimed. "But it should hold together for class!"

"Thank you," Dorrie said happily. "Now I'll wish something nice for you."

"Let's see." Dorrie paused for a very long while. She wanted to give Olivia paint buckets filled with bright colors. But paints could be messy. And she wanted to word the wish exactly right, so that no paint would splatter.

Finally she waved the taped-up wand. *"Olivia needs paint buckets, closed with a top. Make them bright colors. And don't let them plop!"*

Buckets of paint suddenly appeared, hovering over Olivia. Dorrie gasped. The buckets didn't have any lids!

The buckets tipped, and paint slopped over the sides.

Laurel laughed gleefully. "They're going to spill!" she shouted. "Olivia will be covered wing to toe!"

Dorrie gasped. She had goofed again, and she was about to make a mess bigger than anything yet.

In a flash, Trina stepped closer, waving her wand. *"Stop the magic. Paint, don't spill. Stop the magic. Paint, stay still."*

Immediately the buckets froze in place.

"Thanks for helping, Trina." Dorrie bowed her head. "I'm sorry, Olivia. That wish was a disaster."

"That's all right," Olivia said softly. "The spell didn't work because of the broken wand."

"No." Dorrie shook her head. "My spells never work, even when my wand is fine."

"All right!" Laurel said loudly. "I want to grant a wish for everybody!"

Ms. Periwinkle nodded. Laurel waved her wand with a flourish.

"Let's have fun, let's have a ball. Party balloons for one and all."

Colorful balloons floated down from the sky. Spinning . . . bobbing . . . twisting . . . They changed from red to yellow to blue and bounced back up to the clouds.

All the fairies squealed in delight. A first-grader named Sebastian chased a balloon high up in a tree, then batted it to a friend. "Now, that's granting a wish!" he exclaimed. "Everyone loves a party!"

Dorrie sighed. Laurel seemed to do everything just right. And she—Dorrie Lucinda Windmist—did everything exactly wrong.

Chapter 4

When the school bell chimed, Dorrie flew outside. Her mother was waiting for her.

"Mom, what are you doing here?"

"I feel as if I haven't seen you in ages, Dorrie. You spend so much time practicing your dance. So I thought we could take a surprise trip to the Big Dipper for an ice cream treat and spend the afternoon together."

"But won't ice cream spoil my appetite?"

"I won't tell if you won't," her mother said with a wink, and off they flew.

Dorrie absentmindedly twirled her spoon around in her nutshell-bowl. A stream of melted strawberry ice cream shot across the ice cream parlor. "Oops!" said Dorrie. She watched her mother wipe her chin with a napkin-leaf.

Why am I so clumsy that I even make a mess eating? Dorrie wondered. She couldn't help thinking about Laurel. How well she danced. How all her wishes were granted—and how happy she made all the fairy students. Dorrie wanted to do those things too. But how could she, when she couldn't even spoon up ice cream?

"Is something bothering you, Dorrie? You're so quiet," Mrs. Windmist said.

"Well," Dorrie answered, "I want to be a good fairy. But I'm always making mistakes and messing things up."

"Oh, sweetheart, you already are a good

fairy. Who keeps me company when I bake fairy-doodle treats? And who's nice to all the flowers in the neighborhood? And who's my favorite littlest curly-haired fairy daughter? I'll give you one hint—"

"I know, it's me, right?" Dorrie interrupted. She smiled at her mother. "It's nice of you to say those things, Mom, but I can't dance, I fall down all the time, and I can't work my magic wand. What kind of fairy does that make me?"

"It makes you a very special one. When you were less than an inchworm high, your fairy godmother used to say how lucky we were to get such a sweet fairy!"

My fairy godmother! Dorrie thought. Hmmm . . . "Mom, I forgot I have something to do. It's for school. Can I meet you at home?"

"See you there," Mrs. Windmist said. "But don't be out too long. It's a school night."

Dorrie flew out of the ice cream parlor. She

hadn't seen her fairy godmother since she was a baby. She barely remembered her. But surely her fairy godmother would come if she called.

"Now, let's see," Dorrie said out loud. She wrinkled her nose, trying to concentrate. "How should I call her?"

Of course! She could toss a pebble into the babbling brook and make a wish. She raced to Fairy Land Meadow.

✳✳✳

Dorrie picked up a round, smooth stone and fluttered to the talking stream. "Glad to see you!" the brook babbled. "Have you heard the joke about the Big Person? He was so big, when he hurt his toe and couldn't walk, he called a toe truck!"

"Could you please be quiet for a minute?" Dorrie asked. "I'd like to make a wish."

The brook quieted down long enough for

Dorrie to close her eyes, make her wish, and toss her pebble.

Nothing happened except that the brook started to talk again.

"Do you know why six is afraid of seven?" the water babbled. "Because seven ate nine!"

Dorrie sighed. Of course nothing happened. She—Dorrie Lucinda Windmist—had made the wish. And nothing she ever did turned out right. Dorrie flew to the weeping willow tree to see if her friends might be there. They weren't, so she sat under Mr. Willow's droopy branches and felt sorry for herself. Then she spied a root on the ground—the same root that Laurel had tripped over.

If someone as perfect as Laurel could trip, maybe someone as clumsy as I am could be graceful, Dorrie thought.

I'm going to practice the dance again, she

decided. Maybe here, with no one to watch, I'll do better.

"Dum, dum, dum," she hummed. She pointed her toes, then spun around—right into another fairy. They both tumbled to the ground.

Dorrie sat up and stared at the plump fairy, who had a cheerful face. She was as tall as Dorrie's parents and had wild, messy hair.

"Who are you?" Dorrie asked.

"I'm your fairy godmother!"

Chapter 5

Dorrie stared at her fairy godmother. It was almost like looking in a mirror-pond. Her fairy godmother had long curls and chubby cheeks just like Dorrie.

The fairy tried to smooth her hair, then gave up, smiling.

"I don't suppose you remember me. It's been a few sunsets since I last saw you," she told Dorrie. "I'm Lucinda."

"That's my middle name!"

"That's right. I'm so glad we bumped into each other." Lucinda laughed at her joke. "It took me a few minutes to find you. I checked my crystal ball, but it was hard to see where you'd made your wish. I dropped my crystal a few days ago, and it hasn't been the same since!"

The tall fairy held out a smooth glass ball and shook it. The crystal clouded, and it was impossible to see inside.

Lucinda patted Dorrie's wing. "What can I do for you?"

Dorrie thought a moment. Where should she begin?

"My class is supposed to perform the 'Dance of the Sugar Plum Fairy' at our talent show, but I'm a terrible dancer."

"You need help dancing? That's easy! Let's see." Lucinda stood and stretched. "It's been a while, but I think I remember all the steps.

After all, the Sugar Plum Fairy and I went to school together!"

Lucinda held her arms out straight. She bent at the waist. And froze. "Oh, dear!" she cried. "I'm stuck!"

"What?" said Dorrie.

"I have some problems with my back," Lucinda told her, still doubled over. "Ever since I slid down the Rainbow-Bridge and landed flat on my . . . on my . . . Oh, well, you know which end."

"Can I help?" Dorrie asked anxiously.

"Just bend my knees a little . . . there! Now I can sit down. It only takes a few minutes, and then I'll be good as new." Lucinda patted the ground. "You sit down too. We can go over the dance some other time. What else can I help you with?"

Dorrie settled next to her fairy godmother. "We're supposed to end our dance by making a rainbow appear over the audience. But I'm not very good with my wand, and my spells all come out wrong."

"Then let's work on magic. I'll just dig out my wand . . ." Lucinda reached into a deep pocket. "I'm sure it's here somewhere . . ." She pulled out birdseed, feather dusters, and nutshell-bowls filled with purple fish, but no magic wand. "Uh, Dorrie, do you think we could move on to another problem you're having? I seem to have . . . misplaced my wand."

Dorrie shook her head. "It's no use. I'm such a bad fairy even my fairy godmother is mixed up."

"I may not be the most graceful fairy around, and I might lose things every once in a while, but that doesn't mean I'm a bad fairy."

"It doesn't?" Dorrie asked, sniffling.

"No, because—"

"Excuse me, Lucinda." A messenger fairy

hovered by the weeping willow's branches. "Your new crystal ball is ready and waiting at the Magic Glass Shop."

"Oh!" Lucinda glanced at the sun, checking for the time of day. "And it's almost closing time. I'd better hurry." She smiled at Dorrie. "Once I have my new crystal ball, I'll be able to find you in two blinks of a firefly's light. Call me when you need me and we'll talk more."

Lucinda tumbled away from the tree. "Remember," she called back. "Good fairies do more than magic tricks. They make other fairies happy. You don't have to be good at everything to be a good fairy."

That may be true, Dorrie thought, but shouldn't I be good at something?

Chapter 6

Dorrie sat at her desk with a bowl of strawberries for a snack. She was supposed to be studying her spelling book, but she kept thinking about what Lucinda had said.

If being clumsy didn't make you a bad fairy, then Dorrie could still be a good fairy. She'd make everybody happy if she got that rainbow right for the talent show. And that meant working even harder at her magic.

"The only way to get better is to practice," she told herself as she flipped through her spells. "So what should I try? A spell to turn raindrops into gumdrops? Or gumdrops into jelly beans?"

She munched a strawberry. It tasted delicious. She peered into the small nutshell-bowl. Only a handful of tiny berries left, she thought. Too bad there aren't enough for Arianna.

Then she looked back at her book and read, "Make More of Anything."

She grinned. "Aha!" She could practice magic and make Arianna happy. Perfect. She stood up and waved her wand. *"Little berries in the bowl, let's have more to eat. A great big snack that's tasty too, and a great big treat!"*

Dorrie waited. Nothing seemed to happen. Wait a minute! Were the berries growing? Yes! Instead of *more* little berries appearing, the strawberries in the bowl were getting bigger . . . and bigger! There was more to eat—but it wasn't what she had meant at all.

Her magic was mixed up again!

In seconds the strawberries grew too big for the bowl. They covered the desk . . . the floor . . . they were reaching the ceiling!

Dorrie fluttered around and around the giant fruit. How could she stop them? Any minute now, they'd take over the tree-house! She flipped through her spelling book, searching for a reverse spell . . . for a different chant . . . for anything!

"Oh, Dorrie! What did you do now?" a voice asked from behind a giant berry.

"Arianna!" Dorrie sighed with relief. Arianna flew to the ceiling and sprinkled fairy dust. The strawberries shrank to their regular size.

"Thanks, Arianna," Dorrie said. "I was just trying—"

"Forget about it," Arianna interrupted.

She pointed to the combs and barrettes and papers piled into one big heap on her dresser. "What happened here?"

"After you left this morning . . ." Dorrie explained about her search for the fairypack, and the swirling fairy dust.

Arianna sighed loudly. "When will you ever grow up? Big fairies don't lose control of fairy dust. And they don't make giant strawberries by mistake."

"I'm sorry," Dorrie whispered. Her wings wilted as Arianna left the room.

I just wanted to make Arianna happy, but she still thinks I'm a pain in the wing, Dorrie thought miserably. Lucinda doesn't know what she's talking about. I'll never be a good fairy.

Suddenly she brightened. There was one other person she could go to for advice.

Chapter 7

The next morning, Dorrie and her friends flew to school as usual. Once they reached the class branch, Dorrie rummaged through her messy fairypack until she found a lily pad and a feather pen. Then she headed straight to Laurel.

"I think you're a terrific fairy. You get every wish you ask for just right. And you dance the Sugar Plum Fairy dance better than anyone I've ever seen." Dorrie held the pad, ready to take notes. "How do you do it?"

Laurel beamed. "I *am* terrific, huh?"

Dorrie nodded. "I want to be just like you. What's your secret?"

"Wel-l-l-l." Laurel drew out the word. Then she looked around to make sure no one could hear. "I'll tell you because we have so much in common."

"We do?"

Laurel smiled. "We both think I'm terrific! Now, listen carefully. I'm so good at everything because I'm mean!"

"Mean?" Dorrie repeated.

"That's right. Everyone and everything is afraid of me. Stars jump at my command. Birds and bugs do anything I ask. And flowers and trees? Watch this. Hey!" she shouted from the class branch, catching the attention of a nearby daisy. "Give us a breeze!"

Immediately the daisy spun her petals like a fan.

"See?" said Laurel. "And you know what else? You're too nice. That's why you always trip during the Sugar Plum Fairy dance. Other fairies get too close to you and you don't tell them to move. They're always flying in your way. Try to be mean and see what happens!"

Just then Ms. Periwinkle clapped her wings. "All right, class. The talent show is tomorrow. I'd like to spend the morning practicing our dance. Let's go to the meadow."

Great! Dorrie thought. Here's my chance to be like Laurel. The class flew off the branch together and settled on the soft green grass.

"What were you talking about with Laurel?" Belinda whispered.

"Shhh!" Dorrie hissed. She couldn't give

away Laurel's secret. And starting right now, she was going to be mean.

"Excuse me," an ant called, gazing up at Dorrie, "but can you move over an inchworm or two? My anthill is right here, and I'm afraid you'll step on it."

Dorrie shook her head. "No. This is my spot for the dance. And no one is going to make me move."

"Dorrie!" Belinda said, shocked. "That's so mean."

Dorrie caught Laurel's eye. Laurel grinned at her.

A flock of songbirds circled the meadow.

"Whenever you're ready," Ms. Periwinkle called.

The birds flew onto a tree branch, folded their wings, and began to chirp the music for the dance.

The fairies spread their wings. Dorrie bowed with the others. She fluttered her left

wing, then her right. She rose up from the ground.

Olivia swooped close by in a pirouette. "Hey! Watch it!" Dorrie said. "You're getting into my space."

Olivia blushed. "Sorry!" ·

Dorrie whirled around and tumbled into Trina. "You're dancing too close!" she snapped. "Get out of my way."

Then she tripped over her wings and crashed into Belinda. "It's all your fault!" she cried. "Move, Belinda!" A minute later Dorrie scolded Olivia again when they collided in midair.

For the rest of the rehearsal, Dorrie shouted every time someone came close to her. She didn't fall as much as she usually did. But she still had trouble with the rainbow. When she waved her wand, the rainbow quivered and shook and melted like wet candy.

"We still have some work to do," Laurel said. "But not bad for a first try at being mean."

Dorrie walked over to her friends.

Belinda glared at her. "You are the rudest dancer!" she declared.

Dorrie smiled. "I know. But weren't my pirouettes and curtsies better than ever?"

Olivia flung her hair over her shoulders. "I'll tell you what was better then ever. Your pushing and shouting."

"You don't understand." Dorrie wanted to explain why she had acted so mean.

But Trina was already herding Olivia and Belinda away. "You wanted us out of your way," she said over her shoulder. "So we'll give you all the room you need."

Dorrie watched her friends flutter off. They were angry at her!

"Don't worry," Laurel said. "That was just lesson number one. Stick with me and I'll show you how to be even meaner. Then you'll see how good you can really be."

Dorrie looked over at her friends. When she did everything right for the talent show, they'd understand. Wouldn't they? "Whatever you say, Laurel."

✳✳✳

After school Dorrie and Laurel flew to the meadow so that Laurel could show Dorrie another trick. She pointed to a little toad hopping across the grass. "Watch me turn that toad into a handsome fairy prince."

"No, thanks," the toad said, overhearing. "I have to go to the meadow pond now."

"No!" Laurel commanded. She scooped up the toad and held him tight. "I want you to be a fairy prince."

The toad trembled in fear. Dorrie held her breath. This was going too far. Maybe being mean wasn't the answer after all.

"That toad doesn't want to be a prince," Dorrie told Laurel. "I think you should let him go."

Laurel sneered. "No way."

"But my mommy is meeting me at the pond. She's going to give me a bath!" A tear rolled down the little toad's face.

Laurel ignored his pleas. *"Little toad can't go to rinse. He stays right here, to become a—"*

Before Laurel could say "prince," Dorrie knocked the toad out of her arms. "Oops!" she said brightly as the toad scampered away.

"Dorrie!" Laurel cried. "You did that on purpose! I should have known you couldn't be mean. You're just too nice." She made a horrible face. "I'm not teaching you anything else!"

Dorrie was left all alone. She had no friends to practice with, and no Laurel to help her become a better fairy. She'd never master the dance in time, or get the wand trick right for the big finish.

A tear trickled down her cheek. She knew what she had to do. If she told her mom she was sick, she could stay home from school the next day. Then she wouldn't have to be in the talent show. No one would even miss her.

Chapter 8

Dorrie took off to fly home. "Ouch!" she cried as her head bumped something hard.

"Ouch!" yelped someone else.

Dorrie knew that voice. "Lucinda! What are you doing here?"

"I know you didn't call me," Lucinda explained. "But I peeked in my brand-new crystal ball, and saw you looking sad. So I rushed right over. What's wrong, Dorrie, dear?"

"Everything's gotten worse," Dorrie told her. "I'm so bad at dancing and wand-waving, I'll ruin the Sugar Plum Fairy dance for sure. So I'm going to skip the talent show. Then everyone will be happy."

Lucinda pushed Dorrie's hair away from her face and looked into her eyes. "I used to think I was a bad fairy too. But I kept trying and trying."

"I have tried!" Dorrie protested.

Lucinda nodded. "But you've been trying to be like Laurel. You have to be yourself," she said. "And you can't be the best fairy in school all at once. It takes time. And practice. Believe me, Dorrie, I practiced."

"But you still bump into things and fall down. How can you be a good fairy?" Dorrie asked.

"I have a good heart. And I was a good

fairy all along—I just didn't know it. Until one day I was flying home from school and saw my friend, Sugar Plum. She was crying because she thought she was a horrible dancer. Nobody else danced quite the way she did. She felt funny because she was different. I told her she should dance her own special way. It turned out to be quite beautiful. Soon she was performing her dance all over Fairyland. And that's how I discovered my own special fairy gift."

Dorrie felt a little confused. "What *is* your gift?"

"I help fairies believe in themselves so that they can do great things."

"So what great things can I do?" Dorrie asked. "What's my special talent?"

Lucinda began to flutter away. "That's something you have to learn for yourself. But I will tell you this. Don't stay home tomorrow just to miss your dance. Go to school. Trust me."

Dorrie watched Lucinda disappear into the clouds. If her fairy godmother's gift was to help fairies believe in themselves, and she wanted Dorrie to go back to school, maybe she knew something good would happen. But she hadn't been able to say it out loud. There were probably rules against revealing the future.

"All right," Dorrie called after the fairy. "I'll go to school. But I won't promise to dance in the show."

Chapter 9

The next morning, all the fairies were chattering about the talent show.

Dorrie saw her friends hovering above the class branch. She was about to fly over, then stopped. Why would they want to talk to her? She'd been so mean during practice the day before, she wouldn't blame them if they never spoke to her again.

Dorrie dragged her wings and hid behind a leaf, hoping no one would see her.

"May I have everyone's attention, please?" Ms. Periwinkle gazed at her students until they were quiet. "We'll have time for one last practice. We're still having some trouble with the rainbow at the end."

"Excuse me, Ms. Periwinkle?" The principal, Ms. Starshine, fluttered by the tree trunk and beckoned to the teacher. "I'm talking to all the teachers about the show. Could you come with me, please?"

"I'll be right back, class," Ms. Periwinkle said as she flew away. "Try the dance without me."

As soon as the teacher had left, Laurel stood up. "Okay," she said, rubbing her wings. "You know how that rainbow never comes out right because of one clumsy fairy?" She turned around to glare at Dorrie, then smiled brightly at the rest of the class. "I have an idea how to fix it."

"We'll try anything," Sebastian said, and some other fairies nodded.

"Well," Laurel continued, "I'll fly to the front of the stage . . . by myself . . . and wish for the prettiest rainbow ever."

Trina raised her eyebrows. "You'll do it by yourself?"

"Yes. That way it will turn out right."

Trina laughed. "You *think* it will turn out right."

"Look, Ms. Smarty-wings," Laurel said. "I'll prove that I can do it before Ms. Periwinkle gets back. And I'll make it more exciting than a boring old rainbow. I'll wish for rain first, and then the rainbow will appear."

"Wait!" said Trina. But before the word was out of her mouth, Laurel waved her wand.

"Rain, rain, drizzle and drop. Onto our tree branch plop, plop, plop. When rain is done, then for our show, make a beautiful rainbow."

Suddenly huge raindrops pelted down from the sky. They splattered onto the toadstool-desks. But these weren't ordinary raindrops. They were heavy! Each one pounded the class branch like an overgrown pumpkin. The branch dipped dangerously low.

"These aren't ordinary raindrops," Trina cried.

"Oh, no!" Dorrie groaned. Laurel had used too much magic!

C-R-E-A-K. The branch was going to snap off the tree.

Everyone gasped.

"Do something, Laurel!" Sebastian shouted. "The branch is going to break!"

"I can't do a thing," Laurel moaned. "I don't know how to reverse spells!"

"Come on!" Trina ordered the class. "Everybody fly off the branch! That should help."

All the fairies fluttered above the branch. Still it creaked, more and more loudly. The magic rain was more than it could bear.

"We're going to be in major trouble!" Belinda declared.

"Ms. Periwinkle will take us out of the talent show for sure!" said Sebastian.

Everyone would be punished! All because Laurel's spell had backfired and she couldn't reverse it.

Too bad *I* didn't wish for rain. Then we'd have sun for sure, Dorrie thought. All my magic is mixed up. Hey, wait a minute! If I wish for more rain, maybe the sun will come out and dry everything up. I could reverse Laurel's spell!

The branch was sagging so low, it touched the ground. A giant crack appeared. Twigs snapped. Leaves shook and shivered.

It was now or never!

Without another thought, Dorrie began her wish. *"Branch get wet, oh, raindrops come. We want to dance the Sugar Plum!"*

The rainstorm stopped. The sun glowed

brightly. Happy sunbeams streaked toward the tree, drying the desks, the leaves, everything!

Dorrie gazed around anxiously. Ms. Periwinkle would return any second. Would everything be back to normal?

Creak! The branch straightened slowly, rising up, up, up. Leaves lifted, and the toadstool-desks gleamed in the sunlight.

"Here she comes!" Belinda cried, spying Ms. Periwinkle.

"Everyone sit down!" Trina shouted.

The students darted to their seats just as the teacher arrived at the branch. Ms. Periwinkle gazed around. "Okay, class. Everyone up! Let's get that big rainbow finish just right for the talent show dance!"

Chapter 10

The first-grade class flew to the meadow to practice on the soft grass stage.

"What a great spell!" Trina told Dorrie, flying close by. "You saved the day!"

"That's right," Belinda said, giving her a hug. "Thanks to you, we're still in the show!"

Olivia grinned at Dorrie. "Looks like everyone wants to thank you!"

Before Dorrie could say a word about the

horrible practice the day before and how sorry she was, the whole class crowded around. "You're a hero!" Sebastian shouted. Then he clapped a wing over his mouth, afraid Ms. Periwinkle might have heard.

"Dorrie, could I speak with you for a second?" Ms. Periwinkle said. She took Dorrie aside. "I know about the rainstorm."

Dorrie sucked in her breath. Oh, no! Would their dance be canceled after all?

"Don't worry," the teacher said with a smile. "I won't punish the class because of Laurel's mistake. But now you know what being a good fairy is all about: helping people. Not using spells to make friends or impress other fairies."

The way Laurel does, Dorrie thought.

"So," Ms. Periwinkle continued, "you're one of the best fairies I know, Dorrie, because you have a heart of gold."

Dorrie fluttered excitedly around her

teacher. She wasn't just a good fairy—she was a very good fairy.

Then Dorrie spied Lucinda, sitting on a tree branch above the meadow. "Good job!" her fairy godmother called down. "Mixed-up magic can be more powerful than the strongest gift if it comes from a good heart. And now you know your special gift—helping other fairies."

Dorrie smiled as Lucinda settled down to watch the show.

All at once, Laurel stood before Dorrie. "Don't think you're so great, Ms. Dorrie Windmist. You still can't fly in a straight line or dance as well as I do."

"So?" Trina stepped between Dorrie and Laurel and glared at the mean little fairy. "That doesn't mean a thing."

"Laurel," Ms. Periwinkle called, "I need to speak to you for a moment too. About the weather."

"Uh-oh," Laurel muttered as she flew off. Dorrie turned to Trina. "So are we friends again?"

"We never stopped being friends!" said Belinda, flying over with Olivia. "But you have to promise something. Never to try to be like anybody else again. You're too terrific to ever change."

"Dorrie change?" said Arianna, flying by with her class to get ready for the show. "Why should she change?"

"Well, for one thing," Dorrie told her, "you think I'm too messy!"

Arianna grinned. "Sure, you're messy. But I just heard you saved your class branch from disaster. So you must be doing something right, little sister!"

Dorrie was so happy, she danced in the talent show feeling lighter than air. She still made a mistake or two—but no one noticed. And when she waved her wand with her

classmates, a glowing rainbow spread over the meadow. No one really minded that it was upside down!

"It looks like a rainbow smile," Trina whispered.

Dorrie sighed happily. "I guess mixed-up magic isn't so bad after all!"

The Fairy School Pledge

(sung to the tune of "Twinkle, Twinkle, Little Star")

We are fairies
Brave and bright.
Shine by day,
Twinkle by night.

We're friends of birds
And kind to bees.
We love flowers
And the trees.

We are fairies
Brave and bright.
Shine by day,
Twinkle by night.

Here's an exciting chapter from
The Best Book Ever!,
the next Fairy School Adventure!

"Well, hello, fairies," the spider librarian called as they fluttered over. He waved a book in each of his eight arms. Then he shelved them all neatly in a walnut bookcase.

"Guess what, Mr. Spider," Trina said. "We have another book report to do!"

She gazed at the rows and rows of books. She'd read each and every one—twice. None of them were special enough for this report. "Do you have any—"

"New books?" Mr. Spider finished for her.

"I guess I've been asking that question a lot lately." Trina blushed. Sometimes she got bored with the same old fairy tales. "But do you?"

Mr. Spider patted her gently with four arms. "I'm sorry, Trina. Not today."

"That's all right," Trina said. But her wings wilted in disappointment.

Mr. Spider gazed at her for a long moment, thinking. Then he nodded. "Wait here. I may be able to help you after all."

He scuttled away just as Dorrie shouted from across the branch, "Hey, Trina!" She clapped a wing over her mouth. "Oops! Too loud! Can you help me find a book?" she added in a whisper. "There are so many to choose from!"

Trina looked at Dorrie seriously. Should she recommend a book about cleaning up clutter, since Dorrie was always dropping

things and leaving rooms in a mess? Hmmm.
Dorrie had just met her fairy godmother. . . .

"How about the fairy godmother story?
The one where a fairy godmother helps that
Big Person named Cinderella?"

"Great!" said Dorrie.

Trina knew the library so well, she flew to
the right shelf, took the second book from the
left without even looking at the cover, and
handed it to her friend.

"How about me?" asked Olivia.

Trina flew to the art section. Olivia was a
talented artist. She shaped the softest, fluffiest
clouds and carved the prettiest snowflakes.
"Here's one of my favorite books—a collec-
tion of autumn leaves, with suggestions for
mixing fall colors."

"Perfect!" exclaimed Olivia.

Next Trina helped Belinda choose a book
on fairy gymnastics, filled with pictures of
tall, grown-up fairies tumbling from cloud to

cloud, flipping off stars, and sliding down the Rainbow Bridge to Earth-Below.

"Trina!" Mr. Spider called from the back of the branch, hidden by leaves. "I've found something I think you'll like. Come here, please!"

Trina flew past dense twigs and leaves to a room she'd never known was there. Inside, Mr. Spider was blowing dust off the biggest book she'd ever seen. It was so tall, it reached straight up to the next branch.

"I've been saving this book for a long time," Mr. Spider said softly. "My librarian gave it to me after I'd read every book in my school library. I've been waiting to give it to someone who loves books as much as I do."

"Wh-Wh-What kind of book is it?" Trina stammered.

"Why, it's the best book ever! And it's for you!"

rina gasped. The best book ever! And it was hers to keep!

She stared at the cover. It showed a Little Big Person Trina guessed must be in first grade too, sitting on a grassy hill while teeny-tiny fairies fluttered all around. Underneath the words *The Best Book Ever* was another title, *Suzy's Adventures in Fairyland.*

It would be perfect for the book report, Trina realized.

"This is a Little Big Person's book," Mr. Spider explained. "And it's about a Little Big Person. But our best happily-ever-after fairies sprinkled it with special fairy dust. So now a new adventure appears every morning. You can read this book forever."

"A new adventure every day! It's a book that never ends!" Trina smiled. "Can I show my friends?"

"Sure. After all, this book is so big, you'll need help getting it home!"

***

Trina called Belinda, Olivia, and Dorrie into the back room. The fairy friends flitted slowly around the giant book, amazed at its size.

Olivia flew up close to the picture of the Little Big Person on the cover. "She looks nice," she told Trina.

Suzy had short red curls and a big grin that was missing two teeth.

"She does look nice," Trina agreed. "I can't wait to get this book to my tree-house and start reading."

"How should we carry it?" Belinda asked. "It's so heavy, I'm not sure we can fly with it."

"Well, let's try," Dorrie said. She scooted to the top and grabbed a corner. The other fairies took one corner each.

"Ready, set, fly!" said Trina. The fairies flapped their wings, straining with the effort. The book didn't budge.

"Here," said the spider librarian. "Allow me to call some friends." Mr. Spider whistled, and a swarm of bees hurried over.

"Need some help?" the Queen Bee asked. "My workers aren't buzzzzzy at all."

"Yes, please!" said Trina.

The bees whizzed through the air, with the fairies following as quickly as they could. Trina swept past Laurel as the mean fairy was bullying some bees into giving her some honey. Trina could see Laurel's look of surprise as she spied the big book way up in the sky.

Then, in no time at all, the giant book was standing in Trina's backyard.

Belinda settled on the grass and licked one of the honey-sticks the bees had passed around. "Okay, that's done. Now, who wants to go to Fairyland Meadow and slide down the waterfall?"

"Me!" cried Dorrie.

"Me too," Olivia said. She smiled at Trina.

"Are you coming? Or do you want to stay home and read the book?"

"I'm going to stay right here," Trina declared. "Thanks for helping me get it home."

"You're welcome!" the friends chorused as they flew away. "Make sure to tell us about Suzy!" Olivia called back.

"Okay!"

Trina fluttered close to the book, then landed on the cover. She grasped one end and flew in a half-circle, opening it to the first page. "There!"

If you'd like to read more about Trina's adventures with the amazing book, look for

The Best Book Ever!

in a bookstore near you.